A GARFIELD® GUIDE TO ONLINE "FRIENDS"

Not the Same as Real Friends!

Garfield created by
JIM DAVIS

Written by
Scott Nickel, Pat Craven, and Ciera Lovitt

Illustrated by
Glenn Zimmerman, Jeff Wesley, Lynette Nuding, and Larry Fentz

Lerner Publications ◆ Minneapolis

This series will help you learn to stay safe and secure online, from playing games to downloading content from the internet. Use the resources and activities in the back of this book to learn more about cybersafety.

This content was created in partnership with the Center for Cyber Safety and Education. The Center for Cyber Safety and Education works to ensure that people across the globe have a positive and safe experience online through their educational programs, scholarships, and research. To learn more, visit www.IAmCyberSafe.org.

Illustrated by Lynette Nuding & Glenn Zimmerman
Written by Scott Nickel, Pat Craven, and Ciera Lovitt
Layouts by Jeff Wesley, Brad Hill, and Tom Howard
Cover pencils by Jeff Wesley
Cover inks & Colors by Larry Fentz

Visit Garfield online at https://garfield.com/

Lerner Publications Company
An imprint of Lerner Publishing Group, Inc.
241 First Avenue North
Minneapolis, MN 55401 USA

For reading levels and more information, look up this title at www.lernerbooks.com.

Main text font provided by Garfield®.

Library of Congress Cataloging-in-Publication Data

Names: Nickel, Scott, author.
Title: A Garfield guide to online friends : not the same as real friends! / Scott Nickel [and four others].
Description: Minneapolis : Lerner Publications, [2020] | Series: Garfield's guide to digital citizenship | Includes bibliographical references and index. | Audience: Ages 7–11. | Audience: K to Grade 3. | Summary: "Nermal is struggling in his new online game, Cheesequest 7. But when an online friend offers to help him in exchange for his password, Garfield decides to call in Dr. Cybrina, cyber security expert"– Provided by publisher.
Identifiers: LCCN 2019021129 (print) | LCCN 2019980800 (ebook) | ISBN 9781541572775 (library binding) | ISBN 9781541587496 (paperback) | ISBN 9781541583016 (ebook other)
Subjects: LCSH: Garfield (Fictitious character) | Internet and children—Juvenile literature. | Internet—Safety measures—Juvenile literature. | Online social networks—Safety measures—Juvenile literature.
Classification: LCC HQ784.I58 N53 2020 (print) | LCC HQ784.I58 (ebook) | DDC 004.67/8083–dc23

LC record available at https://lccn.loc.gov/2019021129
LC ebook record available at https://lccn.loc.gov/2019980800

Manufactured in the United States of America
1-46544-47589-8/14/2019

AND **I'M** TRYING TO **BEAT THIS GAME,** BUT I KEEP **LOSING!**

ARGHH!

POOR NERMAL. IT'S NOT THE END OF THE WORLD.

NOT THE END OF THE WORLD? OF COURSE IT **IS!** WHAT KIND OF **CHEESE WARRIOR** WOULD I BE...

...IF I CAN'T BEAT *CHEESEQUEST VII: ATTACK OF THE CHEDDAR ZOMBIES,* THE LATEST UPGRADE TO THE WARRIORS OF CHEESE GAME?

ALL FOR CHEESE AND CHEESE FOR ALL!

DING!!!

HEY, COOL!

WHAT IS IT, NERMAL?

ANOTHER **PLAYER** SAYS HE CAN **HELP** ME **WIN THE GAME.** ALL HE NEEDS IS MY **PASSWORD.**

UM, **WHO** IS THIS PLAYER?

HIS SCREEN NAME IS **CHEESE__CAT12.** HE SAYS HE'S AN EXPERIENCED PLAYER AND CAN TOTALLY **HELP** ME WIN. **SWEET!**

Attack of the Chedda

cheese_cat12:
Hey, Nermal! Wanna win this game? I'm an expert! Send me your name and password, and I'll make you an Ultimate Cheese Warrior! :)

MAYBE **NOT** SO SWEET, NERMAL. HOW DO YOU KNOW **CHEESE__CAT12?** FROM **SCHOOL?**

NO, HE JUST **SHOWED UP** ON MY GAME AND SAID HE COULD **HELP.** BUT HE SEEMS REALLY **COOL.**

HE JUST NEEDS MY **PASSWORD** AND **USER INFO** TO HELP ME WIN AND BECOME THE **ULTIMATE** CHEESE WARRIOR!

HMMM, ARE **YOU** THINKING WHAT **I'M** THINKING, GARFIELD?

ARE YOU THINKING ABOUT AN **EXTRA-LARGE PIZZA** WITH **TRIPLE PEPPERONI** AND A **CHOCOLATE-CHOCOLATE-CHIP MILKSHAKE?**

DONUTS DONUTS

NO, GARFIELD! I'M **WORRIED** THAT NERMAL'S GIVING OUT **PERSONAL INFORMATION.**

WHAT SHOULD **WE DO?**

LEAVE IT TO **ME**, ARLENE.

I WAS PLAYING MY NEW VIDEO GAME, **EVIL PIGS FROM PLANET PORKCHOP.** THAT SWINE KING IS A REALLY BAD GUY. SO, WHAT'S UP?

IT'S ABOUT **ONLINE SAFETY.**

PERFECT! AS A **C.I.S.S.P.**—CERTIFIED INFORMATION SYSTEMS SECURITY PROFESSIONAL—I'M ALWAYS ON THE **JOB!**

NERMAL WAS **CONTACTED** IN AN **ONLINE GAME** BY SOMEONE NAMED CHEESE_CAT12 THAT HE **DOESN'T KNOW.** AND CHEESE_CAT12 IS ASKING NERMAL FOR **PERSONAL INFORMATION.**

LIKE HIS **PASSWORD** AND USER **INFORMATION.**

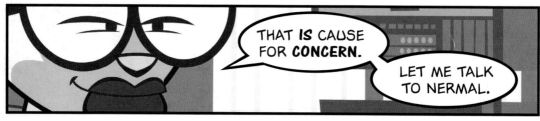

THAT **IS** CAUSE FOR **CONCERN.**

LET ME TALK TO NERMAL.

NERMAL, I HEARD SOMEONE NAMED CHEESE_CAT12 CONTACTED YOU DURING AN ONLINE GAME AND ASKED FOR YOUR PASSWORD AND USER PROFILE.

THAT'S TRUE. HE'S REALLY NICE AND WANTS TO **HELP** ME WIN.

YOU WOULD **NEVER** TELL A **STRANGER** WHERE YOU'RE GOING TO BE OR WHAT YOUR PLANS ARE, SO **WHY** TELL SOMEONE **ONLINE?**

YEAH, BUT HE'S A CHEESE WARRIOR LIKE ME.

ISN'T CHEESE_CAT12 PROBABLY SOMEONE I **KNOW?** OTHERWISE, **WHY** WOULD HE BE WILLING TO HELP **ME** WIN?

MAYBE HE SAW YOUR SCREEN NAME ON THE GAME OR ON SOCIAL MEDIA. BUT REMEMBER, CHEESE_CAT12 IS **NOT** HIS REAL NAME.

IT MIGHT NOT EVEN BE A **HIM.**

IT MIGHT NOT EVEN BE A **KID.**

I NEVER THOUGHT OF THAT.

WE ALL LIKE HAVING FRIENDS,

BUT **ONLINE FRIENDS** ARE **NOT** THE SAME AS **REAL FRIENDS.**

IMPORTANT:

If a stranger contacts you online, tell a parent, guardian, or teacher to make sure you stay safe.

PAWS

IT'S OKAY TO HAVE GENERAL INFORMATION ABOUT YOUR INTERESTS ON SOCIAL MEDIA OR GAMING SITES, BUT YOU WANT TO BE **CAREFUL** THAT A STRANGER CAN'T LEARN **TOO MUCH** ABOUT YOU.

YOU WANT TO **PROTECT** YOURSELF, YOUR FAMILY, AND YOUR FRIENDS.

REMEMBER, NERMAL, JUST LIKE A GREAT CHEESE WARRIOR, YOU'VE GOT THE **POWER** TO KEEP YOUR PRIVATE INFORMATION **SECRET** AND OFF THE INTERNET!

13

LATER THAT AFTERNOON...

IT'S **ANOTHER MESSAGE** FROM CHEESE_CAT12 ASKING FOR MY **PASSWORD**.

GARFIELD, I REALLY, REALLY WANT TO **BEAT** THIS GAME!

HOW ABOUT **THIS?**

I CAN **HELP** YOU BEAT THE CHEESE THINGY GAME, AND THEN YOU CAN **STAY SAFE** AND **SECURE** BY NOT GIVING YOUR PASSWORD TO CHEESE_CAT12.

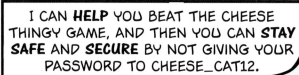

BUT, GARFIELD... YOU **DON'T** KNOW ANYTHING ABOUT VIDEO GAMES... DO YOU?

YOU'VE TURNED THE **ZOMBIES** BACK TO **NORMAL**.

SWEET!!! WE DID IT!

NOW JUST **TWO** THINGS TO DO. LET'S **REPLACE** YOUR **PICTURE** WITH AN **AVATAR**...

CLICK-CLICK-CLICK-CLICK-CLICK-KA-CHUNK!

AND **BLOCK** CHEESE_CAT12!

SO LONG, **WHOEVER** YOU ARE!

cheese_cat12: **BLOCKED!**

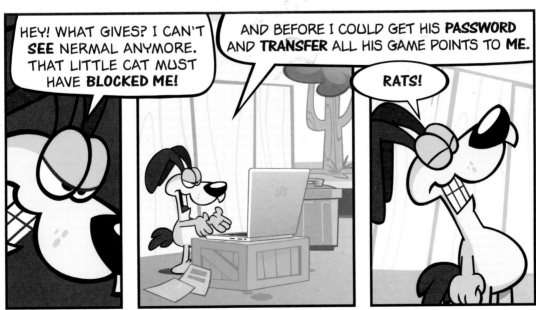

HEY! WHAT GIVES? I CAN'T **SEE** NERMAL ANYMORE. THAT LITTLE CAT MUST HAVE **BLOCKED ME!**

AND BEFORE I COULD GET HIS **PASSWORD** AND **TRANSFER** ALL HIS GAME POINTS TO **ME**.

RATS!

ACTIVITY: OKAY TO SHARE. OR KEEP PRIVATE?

SAY HELLO TO BISBY, MY CYBERSAFETY BOT.

That's B.I.S.B.— Basic Internet Safety Bot—at your service!

B.I.S.B.

Let's talk online safety. Can you figure out what information is private— information you shouldn't give out—and what is okay to share?

PART 1: TO SHARE OR NOT TO SHARE

LOOK AT THE DIFFERENT TYPES OF INFORMATION BELOW. WHICH OF THESE IS OKAY TO SHARE ONLINE? WHICH OF THESE SHOULD YOU KEEP PRIVATE? RECORD YOUR ANSWERS ON A SEPARATE SHEET OF PAPER.

 1. Your Full Name

 2. Funny Jokes

 3. Favorite TV Shows

 4. Phone Number

 5. Your Address

 6. Awards

 7. Your Opinion

 8. Your Password

 9. A Story You Wrote

 10. Your Hobbies

 11. Your Plans

WOW! THAT WAS GREAT!

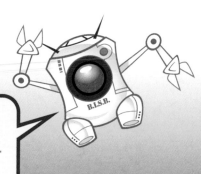

Congratulations! You have just completed part 1. Now, let's see if you can answer a few bonus questions correctly.

PART 2: BONUS QUESTIONS

YES OR NO—IS IT OKAY? RECORD YOUR ANSWERS ON A SEPARATE SHEET OF PAPER.

1. Is it okay to play games online?

2. Is it okay to give out personal information so you can win a prize?

3. Is it okay to give out personal information to my friend's friend online?

4. Is it okay to put up an avatar when I am playing a game or on social media?

Fantastic! You have just completed part 2, the bonus questions. Now, let's take a look at the answers and see how you did.

B.I.S.B.

PART 1: TO SHARE OR NOT TO SHARE ANSWERS

IS IT OKAY TO SHARE OR KEEP THESE THINGS PRIVATE? BELOW ARE THE CORRECT ANSWERS TO THOSE QUESTIONS.

1. Your Full Name – Keep Private

Never tell a stranger or someone you don't know very well your full name. Then they could look up other important information about you or your family and even find out where you live.

2. Funny Jokes – Okay to Share

A funny joke is usually okay to share with someone—as long as it's not about someone else!

3. Favorite TV Shows – Okay to Share

You can share your favorite TV shows because it's just a hobby and something that a lot of people may share.

4. Phone Number – Keep Private

You should never give out your phone number to strangers!

5. Your Address – Keep Private

Your address and the addresses of places you go should be something you never post online and only share with people you've met and trust in real life.

6. Awards – Okay to Share

You can be proud of your achievements—just make sure you don't list anything that could be tracked back to you, such as your school or where your team plays.

7. Your Opinion – Okay to Share

Social media and the internet are great places to express your opinions. Just keep it free of your private information, and what you say should never be mean, offend, or threaten anyone else.

8. Your Password – Keep Private

You should never ever, ever share your passwords with anyone but a parent or guardian. Not even your best friend!

9. A Story You Wrote – Okay to Share

It's fun to share blog posts, or a story you wrote, but you have to be careful because you don't want strangers finding pictures of you or learning too much about you.

10. Your Hobbies – Okay to Share

The internet and social media are great places to share your hobbies! Just make sure you never tell a stranger where you go to practice.

11. Your Plans – Keep Private

You should never tell a stranger your plans, where you're going, who you're going with, and when you'll be somewhere.

PART 2: BONUS QUESTION ANSWERS

YES OR NO—IS IT OKAY TO DO THESE THINGS? BELOW ARE THE CORRECT ANSWERS TO THOSE QUESTIONS.

1. Is it okay to play games online?

Yes. The internet has lots of awesome games. Always ask an adult before playing or downloading a new game. And make sure you don't have to give out any of your private information in order to play!

2. Is it okay to give out personal information so you can win a prize?

No. Contests and prizes are fun, but if you have to share your private information to win, you need to ask your parent or guardian.

3. Is it okay to give out personal information to my friend's friend online?

No. You should never give out any personal information online, including your age or even if you are a boy or a girl.

4. Is it okay to put up an avatar when I am playing a game or on social media?

Yes. You should always use a fun avatar when online. Never use your own picture.

Excellent work. Next, let's help Nermal become safe and secure.

ACTIVITY: STAY SAFE AND SECURE

YOU CAN USE YOUR NEW SAFETY KNOWLEDGE TO HELP NERMAL BE SAFE AND SECURE ONLINE.

STAY SAFE & SECURE

PART 3: MULTIPLE CHOICE

A, B, C, OR D—WHICH ANSWER IS REALLY SAFE AND SECURE? RECORD YOUR ANSWERS ON A SEPARATE SHEET OF PAPER.

1. What should Nermal do first if he doesn't recognize the screen name of someone who is instant messaging him?

A. Ask who they are to find out if Nermal knows them.

B. Answer their question.

C. Try to figure out who they are by pretending to know who they are when talking to them.

D. Tell them that they should plan to meet in person before becoming friends online.

2. What should Nermal do if a friend asks him for his email or social media password?

A. As long as he knows the individual, he can share his password.

B. Nermal should not give out his password to anyone, including his best friends.

C. Nermal should only give the friend his password if he gets the friend's password too.

D. Nermal should give the friend a fake password.

3. What should Nermal do if someone he doesn't know keeps sending him emails or messages, as if they know Nermal?

A. The person must be a friend if they know about Nermal, so just email them back.

B. Nermal should give the person his phone number so he can hear the individual's voice. Maybe that'll help Nermal figure out who the person is.

C. Nermal should tell a parent, guardian, or teacher and get help blocking that person.

D. Nermal should give the person his phone number so they can talk more.

4. What should Nermal do if another kid he talked with on a social media site or message board wants to meet in person?

A. Nermal should discuss this with a parent, guardian, or teacher first.

B. Nermal should tell the kid he has enough friends.

C. Nermal should tell the kid about a party so he can decide if they should be friends once they meet.

D. Nermal should give another friend's address and then watch how funny it is when the kid goes to the wrong house.

5. Nermal got an email from someone whose name he doesn't recognize. What should he do?

A. He shouldn't open or respond to emails from anyone he doesn't know. He should tell a parent, guardian, or teacher.

B. He should forward the email to all his friends to see if they know the individual.

C. He should open it, see what it says, then decide what to do.

D. Nermal should email them back asking for more information.

Wow! Great job. Keep going. You are almost done with the multiple-choice questions.

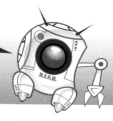

6. What should Nermal do if someone online starts saying weird or mean stuff to him?

A. Say weird stuff back.

B. Ignore it and hope it stops.

C. Tell a parent, guardian, or teacher what the individual is saying.

D. Laugh with friends about it.

7. There's a game online where you can win a cool prize. Nermal just has to type his full name and address so he can receive a prize. What should he do?

A. Nermal should use his name but a friend's address. That'll trick 'em!

B. He should only put in his email address and see if that works.

C. Nermal should enter his information. He could win!

D. He should ask a parent, guardian, or teacher if it's okay.

FANTASTIC! CHECK YOUR ANSWERS ON THE FOLLOWING PAGE TO SEE HOW YOU DID.

PART 3: MULTIPLE-CHOICE ANSWERS

A, B, C, OR D—WHICH ANSWER IS REALLY SAFE AND SECURE? BELOW ARE THE CORRECT ANSWERS TO THOSE QUESTIONS.

1. What should Nermal do first if he doesn't recognize the screen name of someone who is instant messaging him?

The answer is A. Ask who they are to find out if Nermal knows them.

2. What should Nermal do if a friend asks him for his email or social media password?

The answer is B. Nermal should not give out his password to anyone, including his best friends.

3. What should Nermal do if someone he doesn't know keeps sending him emails or messages, as if they know Nermal?

The answer is C. Nermal should tell a parent, guardian, or teacher and get help blocking that person.

4. What should Nermal do if another kid he talked with on a social media site or message board wants to meet in person?

The answer is A. Nermal should discuss this with a parent, guardian, or teacher first.

5. Nermal got an email from someone whose name he doesn't recognize. What should he do?

The answer is A. He shouldn't open or respond to emails from anyone he doesn't know. He should tell a parent, guardian, or teacher.

6. What should Nermal do if someone online starts saying weird or mean stuff to him?

The answer is C. Tell a parent, guardian, or teacher what the individual is saying.

7. There's a game online where you can win a cool prize. Nermal just has to type his full name and address so he can receive a prize. What should he do?

The answer is D. He should ask a parent, guardian, or teacher if it's okay.

NOODLE ON IT!

DISCUSS YOUR THOUGHTS ON THE QUESTIONS BELOW WITH A FRIEND, OR WRITE THEM ON A SEPARATE SHEET OF PAPER.

1. Have you ever felt unsafe online? Why or why not?

2. Have you ever been to a website with an age limit (minimum age requirement)? Why do you think some websites have age limits?

3. Why is it important to keep passwords private?

4. How do privacy settings help keep you safe?

5. What should you do if a stranger talks to you in real life? What about online?

INTERNET SAFETY TOOLBOX

1. Keep personal information private, and do not share it online or in-game.

2. If something makes you feel uncomfortable, log off and tell an adult.

3. Think before you click, send, or post.

4. Create strong, unique passwords, and never share them.

5. Get permission before tagging and posting other people's pictures.

6. Report cyberbullying immediately.

7. Never meet an online-only friend without talking to a parent or guardian first.

8. Follow age rules for social media sites and games.

9. Build safe profile pages, and make sure that your settings are set to private.

10. Remember that online friends are not the same as real friends.

SPECTACULAR JOB! WE HOPE YOU HAD AS MUCH FUN AS WE DID.

Congratulations! You are officially an Online Safety Superstar Extraordinaire!

Be sure to use everything we have learned together and stay safe and secure.

GLOSSARY

avatar: an electronic image that represents a user

block: to ban or restrict a user's access to another user's account

cyber: related to computers and the internet

information systems: systems that interpret and organize information

personal information: information that can help to identify a particular person

screen name: a name used to identify a particular person online

social media: forms of electronic communication through which users create online communities for sharing information, ideas, personal messages, and other content

user info: information, usually a screen name or email address, that identifies a particular user's account and is used to log in to a website

FURTHER INFORMATION

Anton, Carrie. *Digital World: How to Connect, Share, Play, and Keep Yourself Safe*. Middleton, WI: American Girl, 2017.

Being Safe on the Internet
https://kidshelpline.com.au/kids/issues/being-safe-internet

5 Internet Safety Tips for Kids
https://www.commonsensemedia.org/videos/5-internet-safety-tips-for-kids

Hubbard, Ben. *My Digital Safety and Security*. Minneapolis: Lerner Publications, 2019.

Lyons, Heather, and Elizabeth Tweedale. *Online Safety for Coders*. Minneapolis: Lerner Publications, 2017.

Secure Password Tips from ConnectSafely.org
http://www.safekids.com/tips-for-strong-secure-passwords/

Explore more about Cyber Safety at www.IAmCyberSafe.org

INDEX

avatar, 17

block, 17

password, 7, 10–11, 14, 17

personal information, 8, 10–11

screen name, 7, 12

video game, 6–7, 10, 12, 14